WOODY AND JUNE VERSUS THE THIRD WHEEL

WOODY AND JUNE VERSUS THE THIRD WHEEL

WOODY AND JUNE VERSUS THE APOCALYPSE, EPISODE 5

ROBERT J. MCCARTER

LITTLE HUMMINGBIRD PUBLISHING

Woody and June versus the Third Wheel

Woody and June versus the Apocalypse, Episode 5

Copyright © 2019 by Robert J. McCarter

Cover photography © 2018, Robert J. McCarter

"Zombies Ahead" image by ducu59us

Version 1.0, July 2019

ISBN: 978-1-941153-17-8

Find out more about this book at: WoodyAndJune.com

Visit Robert's website at: www.RobertJMcCarter.com

Published by:

Little Hummingbird Publishing

P.O. Box 23518

Flagstaff, AZ 86002

www.LittleHummingbird.com

Little Hummingbird Publishing is a division of Arapas, Inc. Find more about Arapas at: www.Arapas.com.

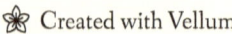 Created with Vellum

CHAPTER ONE

JUNE IS TOYING WITH ME. I can't say that I mind. There's nothing to take your mind off the zombie apocalypse and an escape from dangerous humans like a smart, competent, beautiful woman who you just learned likes boys as well as girls and just might be interested in you.

We've escaped Talia, her ex, who is the psychotic, wannabe warlord that runs the group of survivors down at Phantom Ranch at the bottom of the Grand Canyon. We're on our way up North Kaibab Trail heading towards the North Rim.

Down below, after we managed to escape Talia and her minions, I finally told June how I feel.

And to Talia's credit, I did downgrade her from a "psychotic, *petty*, wannabe warlord" to just a "psychotic, wannabe warlord." June was able to reach her, which is why I am still alive. My forehead still has this strange itch where Talia pressed her gun. It's like I can still feel it there as she threatened to blow my brains out. Just an echo of one of the many post-apocalyptic traumas.

And yes, this is only day eleven of Woody and June versus the Apocalypse, but there is no time to fool around with Zs roaming the land wanting to eat the living, and the living often being a lot more dangerous than the Zs.

The spring day is warm with only high, thin clouds in the blue sky and I'm sweating a lot. June has put on a good pace and I've had to work hard to keep up with her. She's petite, but ex-Army and as tough as they come. We don't have much food, but we've been paralleling Bright Angel Creek so hydration hasn't been an issue.

And I guess that is the problem. There is, literally, no time to fool around. No safety. No peace. No time for anything but survival.

June likes me. She must, right? She's still here even after all our close calls in just a few days. She walked away from Talia with me. And she promised to tell me if there is a chance for us the next time we "have a safe place to rest."

So, what do I do as the miles go by? Search the landscape trying to see if the scraggly desert canyon holds any safety, wonder if there is a secret cavern behind Ribbon Falls that could be safe, wish the few buildings at the campground we pass are far enough from Talia and her militaristic Phantom Company to seem safe. Anything at all.

I wrack my brain trying to remember what's at the top of the trail, but I was a kid last time I was at the North Rim and not really paying attention. There's a lodge and a store, that kind of stuff, but will any of it be considered safe by June?

"We better stop here," I call to June as the trail turns away from the creek and starts up the slope. We're about to leave Bright Angel Creek for the real climb up out of the canyon.

June stops and looks at me, her blue eyes tired but determined. She stands there for a moment, searching the canyon, looking for danger.

And it's what I should be doing with my time. Not fantasizing about safety and her and how everything will change if we could just find some time. I should be focused on survival too.

It's my first rule for each day. Survive. My second is laugh, because you have to have some quality in your life even if you're barely surviving. My new third rule is to spend time with June, because... well... I'm crazy about her.

I turn around and look back, worried that I've missed something.

She walks slowly towards me, her eyes continuing to search, her short black hair sweaty and plastered to her head. I should be searching too, but I find myself staring at her. How can I not. She's got this petite, pixie vibe and is absolutely beautiful.

"We're being followed," she whispers to me as she opens up her water bottle and leans down to the creek to fill it.

"What?" I hiss.

Her eyes widen, and I get the message and lower my tone. "How do you know?" I ask. I plunge my old plastic water bottle in the cold water. Our supplies are very limited. We left Phantom Ranch with almost nothing. Sheets fashioned into slings to carry things, a few granola bars, cheap plastic water bottles, and I've got my trusty Diamondbacks baseball cap, the only thing I've kept since it all went down. Talia had given each of us a gun and a bit more food, but we are not in a good situation.

"I just do," she says. "I've heard a scrape, here or there, that wasn't either of us." She shakes her head. "I just know."

I nod, all thoughts of getting to safety and finding out if the woman of my post-apocalyptic dreams likes me gone. Now I just want to get to safety.

"Talia?" I ask.

June bites her lip. "Not her, not sneaking after us, but she might have sent someone."

I sigh. I guess it's time to add the "petty" back into Talia's title.

"We need to drink as much as we can here," I say in a normal conversational tone in case we are being overheard. "We are about to head up and won't have access to water."

June gives me a weak smile and nods, taking a deep drink.

"We got this," I whisper, but I'm not sure I believe it.

CHAPTER TWO

WE DIG INTO THE SWITCHBACKS, shortening our strides but keeping our pace steady. The rocks and the dirt of the trail are iron rich and all have a red hue. It's spring and it's in the mid-seventies here, but with this climb that's hot. We've got our jackets tied around our waists. It's awkward, but you never leave a jacket behind—you *will* always need it at some point.

And my dull green army surplus jacket has my packs of seeds in the inside pocket. Not a ton, just some beans and vegetables that I took when I left Phoenix. Those seeds represent the future and the ability to grow food and be self-sustained.

I know it's more symbolic than anything, but those two things, my hat that links me to my past and the seeds, which point to the future, help keep me sane.

We're just past Redwall Bridge that takes you over a narrow but steep bit of canyon. We debated bushwhacking around and waited off the trail for a while to make sure it was clear. It's a wood decked metal bridge like the one over the Colorado River, but much smaller. We ended up going across one at a time, but between the bridge not feeling safe and June's conviction that we're being followed, it's been a bit tense.

Well, that and the whole escape from Talia and living in a world terrorized by zombies. Yeah, that too.

"I have a plan," I say, pulling up next to June.

She looks amused, briefly, and I'm relieved. Given our history with my plans I'm glad to see it. "Care to explain," she says, her voice low so as to not carry.

I nod and give her the best smile I can. "There's a place called Supai Tunnel coming up. If we are being followed that's the place to find out."

"A tunnel?" she asks.

"Yeah. It's the only way up, you have to go through it."

"A good place to ambush our follower is a good place to ambush us," she says.

My smile disappears, I hadn't thought of that. "We'll be careful."

She nods, all grim determination, and my determination is to lighten things up.

Sure, someone might be following us, but I don't think their intent is to do us immediate harm or wouldn't we have been shot at by now? And yes, we are in the middle of a zombie apocalypse, but we haven't seen a Z since we hit Phantom Ranch, and if they are around here, they must be few and far between.

But what about that zombie tourist herd on the South Rim that chased us down into the canyon, you might ask. Well, the North Rim is isolated and hard to get to. I am sure there are Zs, but there can't be that many and I don't see a horde of them randomly traipsing down the trail.

"So... I've been thinking about your Gaia theory of the origin of the Zs," I say in between breaths as we wind up the switchbacks.

She glances at me briefly and says, "Ummm hmmm."

"That was Talia's idea, right?" Talia is this weird combination of evangelistic Christian and earthy goddess lover, invoking both Jesus and Gaia pretty often.

June stops, her eyes searching mine, and then she takes a sip of water. "What are you getting at?" Even her breath is coming fast as we climb.

I shrug. Truth is this tact wasn't well thought out. I thought that discussing my time travel theory of the apocalypse versus her Gaia theory might be amusing, but I've taken us right back to her ex. "Umm... just trying to understand it," I say, attempting to recover. "Trying to understand her. You know, in case..." I nod back down the trail.

June's eyes linger on mine as if she thinks there is more there and if she looks at me long enough she'll either divine it or I'll spill—the latter is actually quite likely. She stows her water bottle in her sheet sling and nods. "Yes, her theory, but it works better than yours." She turns and marches up the trail.

"Better?" I ask. "How is a conscious planet better than our far future ancestors trying to stop us from ruining the planet, or benevolent aliens trying to stop us from destroying our race?"

She snorts and that makes me smile. "First off, your aliens and ancestors are both sadistic bastards laying this crap on us."

"And Gaia isn't?"

She shakes her head. "No. Think of the planet as a single organism and we are cells that make up that organism. Did you feel bad when you lost a few pounds after the holiday, wiping out millions of fat cells?"

The trail is wide enough so that I can walk next to her and I try to catch a glimpse of her face. There is a bit of a smile playing there. She's messing with me and that's a good sign.

"And," she continues, glancing at me, those blue eyes a bit brighter, "you have to contend with the impossibility of time travel and the huge difficulties of interstellar space travel with your theories."

"And you have to explain a conscious planet," I counter.

She shrugs. "Easily done. Explain how the individual neurons in your brain coalesce into consciousness and I'll explain how the individual, seemingly disparate, beings on this planet create a consciousness."

"But wouldn't we be aware of that? Wouldn't we know that?"

She shakes her head. "Does one neuron in your brain know of the larger whole it is a part of?"

"Well... I'm a little more complicated than a single neuron." My tone is defensive now. I've lost my intent in this conversation and am just in it.

"Then prove it, and wrap your brain around the possibility."

"Aliens are more fun," I counter.

She stops, her arms crossed awkwardly over her sheet sling pack thing. "What the hell about this is fun? Answer me that, Woody? We need water. We need food. We need shelter. How many times in the last week have we almost bought it? Where the hell is the fun?"

I'm panting hard from the exertion and from the adrenaline of our little argument. Really, our first argument. She has a point; the particulars of our survival are not very fun. But that misses the larger point. A life needs to be worth living, even a post-zombie-apocalypse life.

"Meeting you, that was fun," I say quietly. "When you taught me to shoot by the Little Colorado River Gorge, that was fun... you know, except for the gun part." At this she smiles, briefly, knowing how much I hate guns, but maybe seeing that her teaching me is what made it fun for me. "Rafting down the Grand Canyon, even though we were prisoners, that was fun."

The smile is gone and yet her eyes are wide and she's blinking too much. I think Talia and our close call added to the worry about being followed may have pushed her past her limit. She has limits, which is both comforting and scary at the same time.

"Holding hands with you," I continue, "anytime and anywhere is fun." I hold my hand out and she takes it.

And yes, I am an unabashed, unashamed romantic. Before I met June, I wasn't wanting to interact with any humans, much less an amazingly competent—and yes, beautiful—woman.

"Hiking the Grand Canyon, just you and me," I continue. "This is fun." She opens her mouth to speak, but I forge on. "I know it's serious. I know our survival is tenuous. I'm not dumb. But for me fun is doing the things I want to do, not the things I have to do. And being with you is what I want to do. It takes this existence beyond survival into a life worth living."

She's blinking again and nodding, her eyes wide.

It's a moment. The world is quiet around us, just the barest of breezes and the chirping of birds. I want to kiss her, so much. We aren't safe, exposed on these switchbacks, but it's clear that no one is near. My nose if full of her sweet and sweaty scent. I lean down and she doesn't turn her head away. I move in to close the distance and—-

"Shit!" she hisses, turning her head away. "Did you hear that?"

I think back and do recall a scrape a moment ago, like a foot slipping on a rock.

I straighten up and nod. And then I hear a rock bouncing down the slope below us.

The moment has passed. It's time to figure out who is following us.

CHAPTER THREE

I USED TO BE A WAITER. Hours on my feet taking orders, regurgitating details of the menu, hauling food, dealing with stupid requests and thousands of different diets, hoping for decent tips. It wasn't bad work, not in the least. I spent some time working construction, and being inside away from the Phoenix heat made it vastly superior, but I always felt trapped by it, by the need to make money.

I'd spend all the best hours of my day doing something I had to do, not something I wanted to do. It seemed like that job, and all similar jobs, were just leaching my life slowly away until one day I would wake up old and decrepit, no longer able to work, the world having sucked me dry.

The Zs changed all that and made each day a struggle for survival. You have to find food and shelter. You have to survive the Zs, the environment, and the psychotic, petty, wannabe warlords and their merry bands of sadists.

It makes it hard to relax, hard to breathe sometimes, but there seems to be a reason for everything.

I ponder this as we wait for our pursuer on the other side of Supai Tunnel. I think we would have agonized over going through it, worrying about an ambush, but we didn't have time. Besides, Talia was so confident about catching us down there, she wouldn't have sent someone up in front of us. And I wasn't worried about an ambush from above, this was still the territory of Phantom Company.

In the end, I just walked through to June's objections.

The tunnel is an even better spot for ambush than I had thought. It is about twenty feet long, sloping up through the red rock and curves a bit at the end. It then opens up to a flattish area that has some pit toilets, a water fountain for thirsty hikers—that no long works, of course—and long hitching posts made out of metal pipe to tie the mules to that used to drag tourists down here. The ones that didn't want to hike the two miles down—or really up, it's a 1400-foot elevation gain, so not just a walk around the block.

June is positioned on the right side of the trail and will see our pursuer first, and since she can actually shoot that gun she's holding, I offered no objections. I'm to the left and we're both crouched behind large sandstone boulders that provide decent cover.

The curve in the tunnel means we won't be able to see anyone until they are almost all the way through—it also means they won't be able to see us.

You could try to use that bend as cover and shoot your way out, so we're both squatting there with our guns out.

We're almost to seven thousand feet in elevation now, and since we've stopped moving, I'm finally cooling down.

At this point, there is no doubt about the pursuer. They are there, on the other side of the tunnel, and my heart kicks into high gear.

We can't see to through to the other side, but I heard the footsteps and I heard them stop and can dimly hear rapid breaths. It sounds like one person and they were moving fast, trying to catch up to us, I'm sure.

I throw June a worried look with a short nod, kind of an "Oh shit, you called it" look and she returns a grim smile, her gun in hand.

I have my gun too, but still really hate the thing. If it comes down to gunfire, I will be a distraction, June will be the one that actually hits something.

Minutes drag by and it's silent except for the breeze and the cawing of some ravens, the sound bouncing around the canyon eerily. The smell of the mules that tarried here still lingers, a vague acrid scent, the ground overused by them for too long and nature has not had time to properly reclaim it. Like much of civilization, their presence lingers even as it fades. A fly buzzes me and I shoo it away, it is probably longing for the mules and its easy food source to come back.

This doesn't have the banality of being a waiter, that's for sure. It's got the adrenaline of survival. I could use the banality of a soul-sucking job right now.

Five more minutes tick past and still nothing. Whoever it is, they are being careful. Do they suspect we are waiting in ambush? They must.

June's eyes are fixed on the tunnel and I'm getting antsy, about to say something when I hear crying. A child... no, a woman crying. At first, I can barely hear it and then it gets louder, but still restrained. The kind of sobbing this zombie-filled world can bring on.

The sound echoes through the tunnel and I blink, my heart heavy. I've sobbed just like that, many a night alone, barely holding on, not knowing what's next or how I'm going to keep going, much less survive.

And then the sobbing intensifies into more of a wail before it suddenly cuts off. "I'm coming through now," she says with a sniff, her voice echoing in the tunnel. "I'm unarmed. Please don't shoot."

June steadies herself and levels her gun, but I stand up, my gun in my hand, but at my side.

Like most males, the sound of a woman crying is a complicated and terrifying thing. And yes, this might be a tad misogynistic, but it makes me want to lend aid, to help, to make it better. If a man cried, I think my reaction wouldn't be as nearly as compassionate. I'd be more "suck it up" than "what can I do to make you stop crying?"

Yup. My discomfort with women crying is all about me. And I get all that, but it runs pretty deep.

I have a hard time imagining June crying, but this woman, whoever she is, needs help.

June stabs a look at me, but I don't sit down.

"It's okay," I yell. "Come on through. We won't shoot."

"Sit down, Woody," June hisses. "Now!"

I shake my head, but don't leave my shelter like I would have on my own. I just stand there like a dope, the perfect target for Talia's mercenary sent to get rid of the competition so that June goes running back to her.

The thought lands on me with a nearly audible thud. Well, at least my gasp is audible as I realize what has always been clear to June. Just as the woman appears in the tunnel, I duck back behind my cover, convinced that she is here to kill me. That she cried like that figuring I had the usual straight male phobia to females crying and was using me.

It's clear when it comes to survival, having women around makes it more of a challenge. My constant being distracted by June and "what might be" and my stupidity just now with this complete stranger proves it.

The woman walks through the tunnel and my heart pounds out a syncopated rhythm in my head. Was her crying real? Is she here to kill me? Why would Talia send someone after us right after making such a show of letting us go?

And then recognition hits. I've seen her before.

CHAPTER FOUR

SHE'S around thirty with shoulder-length brown hair and a round face. She's tall and pretty with a few extra pounds, which is unusual to find these days.

Her left knee is a bloody mess as well as her right hand; she must have taken a good spill. She doesn't appear to have anything on her, no gun, no pack, no water bottle. She's dressed in khaki shorts and a grey tank top.

"I... Please don't shoot," she says, her eyes red rimmed, making it look like the crying was real.

"Who are you?" June asks, standing, moving onto the trail, her gun pointed at the woman's chest.

"Dallas. My name is Dallas... I... I escaped in the chaos back there. Please... please don't shoot."

I stand and walk up next to June, my mind a mess. In the old days, pre-June, I would have avoided the encounter, hidden, stayed on my own. My little assassin fantasy, while plausible, was crumbling in the presence of this clearly distraught person.

"You, over there," June points with her gun and the woman walks into the open area next to the metal hitching post. "Woody, keep your gun on her, shoot her if she moves. I'm going to check the other side of the tunnel."

June moves carefully into the tunnel, I hear her footsteps echoing out, but I'm focused on Dallas. She's pretty, with brown eyes and noticeable smile lines.

"I remember you," I say. "You were one of the sentries down at Phantom Ranch. You came in for breakfast after everyone else was done."

I have this clear memory of being in the dining hall at Phantom Ranch and her looking at me intently and smiling. It was one of the few kind looks I got that day. But it was more than a smile and a look; both seemed to have a heat behind them like she was flirting with me.

She nods and bites her lip. "Talia's crazy. I hated that place, but never saw a way out until..." She nods at me, referring to the fire we started as a distraction so we could get away.

I glance at the tunnel but don't see June. I'm sure she's seeing if there is anyone else here.

"You were a sentry, why didn't you just leave one night?"

She shrugs. "We are rarely alone, and how would I survive out here all by myself?"

"How did you get past Talia, Sal, and Harris after they let us go?"

She smiles shyly. "It was dark. I hid until after they passed."

I don't know if I believe her, but I could believe it was chaotic enough last night for someone to slip out. And she has nothing, which lent credence to it being unplanned, not to mention her injuries.

"All clear over here," June calls from the tunnel.

"I'm alone..." Dallas began. "Please... I..." Her eyes well up with tears and I feel that compulsion to help again. I fight it down as best I can.

"What are we going to do?" I whisper to June when she gets back next to me.

She takes a deep breath, her eyes fixed on Dallas, her gun pointed at her chest. "We have to take her with us," June says. "We can't have her running back to Phantom Ranch and we can't have her following us."

I nod. I don't like it, but I don't see any other options.

June pulls a water bottle out of her sheet sling. It's only got about an inch of water left, but she tosses it to Dallas. "We can't have you falling over from dehydration."

"Thank you," Dallas says, and quickly drains the water.

"Get going now," June says. "Stay on the trail, don't try to run or I will shoot you."

She nods. "Thank you. Thank you both." She starts walking slowly up the trail and we follow when she's about twenty feet ahead.

"Do you think Talia sent her?" I whisper.

June snorts and raises her eyebrows, nodding her head.

"What are we going to do?" I ask.

"Get out of this damn canyon and then you're going to find us some shelter."

I nod and pull my beat-up map of the Grand Canyon out of my pocket, wishing I remembered the North Rim better than I did.

CHAPTER FIVE

THE SOUTH RIM of the Grand Canyon sits at seven thousand feet and perches over the gorgeous erosion near the river. The North Rim, on the other hand, is up above eight thousand feet and is spread among side canyons that cut deeply to the north.

The South Rim is easy to get to, full of tourists, with the overlooks close together. The environment is desert-like.

The North Rim is hard to get to, far fewer tourists, with long drives between overlooks as you thread from one side canyon to another. The environment is more forested, with the pine trees and a few spruce and fir right to the edge.

For both of these reasons, the forest and the isolation, I love the North Rim.

This difference between the rims is caused by geology, the land sloping from the north down towards the south, causing rainfall at the South Rim to flow away from the canyon, while rainfall at the North Rim flows into the canyon, producing the deep side canyons.

The three of us are standing in the parking lot of the North Kaibab Trailhead. We are fourteen miles from Phantom Ranch, it's late afternoon, and we are tired, hungry, and dehydrated.

There's an outhouse here, which we've all taken advantage of, and a sloped parking lot for about forty cars that is about a quarter filled. That's the advantage of simple things, like pit toilets, they still work even after civilization is gone. Although they would have worked better had there been some toilet paper left.

Dallas had been quiet, trudging ahead of us up the final switch-backs, it's the kind of climb that is hard enough to make most everyone quiet, but she has more reasons than that. She's got some kind of tattoo under her tank top. I see a beak and maybe feathers peeking out. We need to know more about her, but I don't think either June or I have had the energy. We just escaped Talia, lack supplies, and are in a bad spot again.

This would be much simpler without Dallas.

"What now?" Dallas asks, looking directly at me. June is looking at me too.

Who put me in charge?

"How much does Phantom Company come up here?" I ask Dallas, trying to sound confident, but it's the first thing that popped into my head.

"Plenty, with the huge herd that was on the South Rim, but I've never been out of Phantom since I arrived."

So, it's probably picked clean. A lack of food we might have to deal with, but we need to find water and shelter.

"Do you think they'll send someone after her?" I ask June.

She pointedly looks at Dallas instead of answering.

Dallas scrapes her hiking boot on the pavement, her head down. She takes a deep breath and lets out a noisy sigh. "She... Talia. She wanted to... to date me." She looks up and her eyes are haunted. "I worked in the kitchen then and turned her down, that's when I got put on sentry duty."

I'm about to ask about that when June does. "Sentry duty? Seems like a promotion?"

Dallas snorts. "Guarding gates all night, every night, never alone, bored to death, sleeping when most everyone else is awake?" She shakes her head. "No. It was punishment."

"So, do you think she'll come after you?" I ask.

She looks down at her shoes again. "She's crazy, you know. Obsessed. But it's not me she wants now."

June blinks and nods. She's still got her gun out, but the miles and this story seems to have mellowed her about Dallas. It's a story June can relate to.

And then they're both looking at me.

"Okay. A plan," I say, making it up as I go. "Let's go slow and systematic. We need transportation, so let's check these cars, and while we're at it, let's see if they have anything useful—and considering how little we have, that might just actually be possible—and then we'll head for the lodge."

June guards us with both of our guns, and Dallas and I start picking through the cars. There's about ten of them and they're a mess. They've been open to the weather with broken windows, popped trunks and hoods, dried pine needles inside, and seats chewed up by squirrels.

"How did you end up down there?" I ask as we're rooting through a minivan. I find a tire iron and grab it, any weapon in a zombie apocalypse, as the saying goes. And yes, that really is a saying if you're reading this long after the zombies are gone—I gotta have hope, you know. Anything that will stop the fungus heads from eating you is welcome. Anything that helps you survive, a blessing.

"Just an accident," she says. "I was in Holbrook holed up in an old hotel—the thing had fake teepees, for God's sake—when Talia and her group came through. I ran into them when I was scrounging and was 'recruited.'"

She shakes her head, sweeping pine needles out of the side of the van while I'm rooting around the back. I understand what she means by "recruited." Talia finds you and you're a part of the group even if you don't want to be.

I find a Bic pen, shove it into my pocket. I remove the gas cap and there isn't even a whiff of gas so we move on to an old sedan and then a Jeep Cherokee. I'm checking the cars and searching, but keeping an eye on Dallas too. She is quick and thorough, looking everywhere. She finds a pair of sunglasses in a little cubby and puts them on, but that and the pen and tire iron are the only things besides pine needles, scat, empty gas tanks, and trash we find.

While Dallas starts on another car, I eye up the trash cans up by the outhouse. They are off-white metal rectangles with sloping tops one is for trash, the other for recycling with the tricky lids to keep bears out.

"Nothing?" June asks, still keeping a good distance from Dallas and me.

I brandish my tire iron. "Not a bat, but I'll take it. I think Phantom Company drained the gas out of these long ago and scavenged them for parts." I point to the trash cans. "Might as well be thorough."

I use my superior human hand and push open the latch, the "how to" illustration still sticking tenaciously to the lid. Inside I find, you guessed it, trash and recycling—for reasons beyond me, humans didn't seem to be able to put trash in the trash can and recycling in the recycling can, although they could obey the instructions on how to open the lid. It doesn't stink—any garbage dumped in here has long rotted away. It does have this stale musty smell, though, which reminds me of the Zs.

I pull out some decent water bottles with lids, all empty, and put them in my sheet sling and go to the next dumpster. I get some empty bottles for June and Dallas and find some paper with one side blank and fold it up and put it in my pocket.

"Hey!" Dallas shouts, pulling a dirty backpack from underneath the car she was searching. It's filthy but was once pink with a big Hello Kitty on the back.

I signal her over and we stuff the little backpack full of empty water bottles.

"Let's move on," I say, signaling Dallas in the direction of the lodge. Her brown eyes lock with mine and I feel guilty for still treating her like a prisoner. She holds my gaze for a breath and then sighs, her shoulders slumping.

The parking lot slopes down to the road which then curves up and around a large tree-covered hill, kind of a switchback for cars and I know we are all sick of switchbacks. There's a nice dirt path paralleling the road, but without cars on it, the road is a lot safer. "Let's stay on the road, more open," I say, even though Dallas is already headed towards the road.

She starts walking in front of us. She's our prisoner and I hate it. I don't want to be a psychotic, petty, wannabe warlord bossing people around at gunpoint. I don't want to petty, or psychotic, even. I just want to survive.

And right now, the only thing we have in abundance is empty water bottles. We need water and food and a vehicle. We likely haven't seen the end of Talia and need to leave the area. Now.

June's blue eyes narrow and catch mine as if to ask, "Are you okay?"

I smile, as best I can, and nod. "Let's see what we can find at the lodge."

CHAPTER SIX

FROM THE TRAILHEAD, the road heads west, snakes up and around a big hill through a thick forest of ponderosa pines with firs mixed in and a few aspens, and then heads south towards the lodge and Bright Angel Point.

The road is post-apocalyptic, meaning it is untended and covered in debris. Dirt and pine needles cover much of it as if the forest is reaching out and trying to reclaim the road. There are large tracks of dried mud and stones where heavy rains flowed mud onto the road. There is evidence of vehicles, tire tracks through the dirt, but not that many and not that often.

As soon as we crest the hill and start heading south, a Z comes shambling forward from off the road near some buildings that I can just glimpse through the trees. The building doesn't look familiar; it's been a long time since I was here.

We just passed Admin Loop on the right, that is where the back-country office is and housing for the people that worked here. This other building is big and brown with a green roof, up ahead on the left.

"I'll get 'em," I call cheerfully, jogging ahead of Dallas with my tire iron.

Truth be told, I'm tired, hungry, exhausted, and desperate for some rest, but Dallas doesn't have a weapon and I don't want June shooting—too much noise.

The Z stinks of rotting flesh with a moldy keynote, like they all do, but he's in good shape with torn jeans and a denim jacket. His face isn't desiccated at all and he only has a gash on one cheek. He's also a bit slower and clumsier as new Zs tend to be. Strange.

It's snarling and snapping its jaw, its teeth clacking. I kick it in the chest, it goes down. I stand on its chest and it claws at my jeans. I use the sharper end of the tire iron and shove it through his eye socket and one more Z is taken care of. Only about six billion to go.

I stand up and smile at June and Dallas, sure what we need right now is a moment of humor. "How many Zs does it take to screw in a lightbulb?" I ask.

June rolls her eyes and shakes her head.

"How many...?" Dallas asks tentatively, as if she's worried there is something sinister behind my question.

"They won't do it," I say, pointing at the now still zombie. "They lack the brains!" I draw "brains" out in total B-movie style. "Braaaaiii-innnnssss."

June groans, but Dallas laughs. It's awkward, a bit of a giggle, but at least there's some kind of laughter today.

"Don't laugh," June says to her, "you'll just encourage him."

"Why shouldn't you ever go to a zombie doctor?" I ask, sufficiently encouraged.

June's still shaking her head, but smiling now. "Why?"

"Because his diagnosis is always the same... there's something wrong with your braaaaiiiinnnnssss!!!"

June chuckles and Dallas laughs for real. These are bad jokes, not really worth the laughter, but these are desperate times. Any joke in an apocalypse. And no, that one's not a saying yet, I just made it up.

I'm pulling the denim jacket off the Z when Dallas says, "Wait... wait... I've got one."

I look up. "Let's have it."

"What do a scarecrow and a zombie have in common?" Dallas asks, a big smile on her face.

"What?" June asks. June is clearly enjoying this silliness, but she's still got her gun in her hand and is still keeping her distance from Dallas.

"Their favorite song is 'If I only had a *brain!*'"

We all laugh, but it doesn't last long. The silence and stillness of the world seem to descend heavily. There's no road noise, no voices, no people.

It's just us the three of us on North Rim of the Grand Canyon with a psychotic, petty, wannabe warlord that is obsessed with June, and we have no way of escaping.

I get the jacket off the Z and toss it to Dallas. "It's going to be cold tonight," I say. "You're going to need this." The Z has a knife on his belt and I take both the knife and the belt, again wondering what a new zombie is doing here. I search the body, but there is nothing else worth taking.

When I stand back up, June is looking at the building where the Z came from. It's a tall L-shaped building with brown walls, a green roof, and several large garage doors. Behind it are two towering water tanks.

"Okay," I say, heading down the road to the building. There is really no choice—we need water.

In front of the building are two signs. One is brown with a half-circle of colors going from green to red and a pointer. It says "Grand Canyon National Park. Fire Danger Today." except some joker scratched out "Fire" and carved in "zombie." The needle is pointed to "Low". The second sign says "Grand Canyon. North Rim. Emergency Services". It's made of wood, with the letters carved in as well as the National Park Service logo.

With the building's size and huge bay doors, it makes me wonder how many emergencies they were having up here. No doors are open and there are no vehicles in the semi-circular driveway or near the building.

I start down the far portion of the driveway past the signs, but June doesn't follow, she's staring at Dallas who is still on the road holding the jacket I gave her, a blank look on her face.

I walk back to June. "What do we do with her?"

She shrugs.

Dallas may be telling the truth, that she escaped Phantom Ranch in the chaos, or she might have been sent by Talia to... Well, I'm not sure there. Talia wants June, so Dallas could be here to kill me so June goes running back to Talia. That doesn't make sense, June wouldn't do that and Talia knows it.

Dallas is looking scared, her brown eyes wide as she studies us studying her. She's competent, but that is pretty much to be expected at this point post apocalypse.

We could tie her hands, similar to what Sal and Mary did to June and me when they captured us down in the Grand Canyon and cuffed us together, but I don't know if I can do that. If her intent is innocent, if she really is just trying to escape, that's not right.

And if her intent is not innocent? I don't know, but leaving someone with their hands tied to fight off hungry zombies doesn't seem like the kind of thing that is ever right. Maybe since I've experienced fighting Zs while restrained, I'm extra sensitive here.

"We have a trust issue," I say, nodding back to the building. "There could be more Zs back there, but we need the water. We need to move quickly, stay alive, and find a way out of here, and that is going to be hard if we don't trust you."

Dallas nods and shrugs. "What can I do?"

And there really is nothing. Trust comes with time. It has to be demonstrated. June and I trust each other even though we haven't been together long because we have good reason to.

I look at June and she is clearly worried. If it was anyone but Talia that was the threat, I think she would have been much more assertive. She did, after all, fake her own death by zombie to escape Talia.

"We're going to check this place out," I say. "I suggest you stay out here, watch, come get us if you see anyone or anything coming."

I grab a stick, pull out my multi-tool, flick open the knife blade, and quickly sharpen the edge and toss it over to her. "Just in case."

Dallas picks up the stick, nods, and frowns. "But don't get too close to you guys, right?" she asks.

"Exactly."

June nods, hands me my gun, and we go in.

CHAPTER SEVEN

IT SEEMS like I've done this thing a thousand times. This is life now. You approach the unknown, slowly and warily, you map out your escape routes, you stay quiet and use your ears, you breathe deep through your nose so you can smell the Zs. You feel scared and excited at the same time, your heart rate elevated, your senses sharp.

The forest is quiet, just a breeze through the pine needles, some squirrels scrambling up a tree, and the cawing of the ravens that are all over the place up here.

The building looks to be in good condition, the shorter portion of the L jutting toward the road is all large bay doors like you'd see at a fire station, the right side of the building has large vehicle doors too. I imagine fire trucks inside and for a brief moment want to go find out, go fire one up and let the siren blare, chasing away the eerie silence. But it is only a moment, water is what we need.

June and I stay about five feet apart, we don't talk about it, it just feels natural.

We slowly circle around. There's a shed to our right past two large dumpsters and the two large water tanks in back.

This is the first pass, we aren't getting aggressive, we are just looking, listening. Are there Zs here? Are there people here?

When we're out of sight of the road and Dallas, I nod towards the water tanks. "Let's circle around those too."

The tanks are huge, maybe ninety feet in diameter and twenty-five feet tall. They're painted a fading green and were clearly the water supply for the North Rim. There used to be a chain link fence around them, but someone removed it, leaving just the metal posts sticking up. I suspect that Phantom Company gets their water here when they are up.

June nods and we widen our path and slow down even more. The forest is thick and grows close to the tanks, the hill we followed the road up dropping off not far behind, our feet crunching on twigs and dried pine needles.

When we are back behind the right-most tank, I touch June on the arm and quietly say, "Do you think Talia sent Dallas?"

June's eyes scan our surroundings before meeting mine. "Good odds."

"And what is she here to do?"

"Separate us. Drive us apart. Remove the competition."

I'm staring at her, blinking. I mean, June is amazing and competent and beautiful. I can see how she is desirable. I can see how Talia would view me as the competition, but...

"Shit!" June hisses, squeezing my arm.

It's a group of five zombies shambling towards us. These look brand new too, like the one on the road. What the hell?

"No guns," I say, no longer bothering to whisper. "We don't know what else is around here."

June nods and we start moving back the way we came, out of the forest into the lot surrounding the building.

"Let's lead them out to the road," June says, "see what Dallas can do."

I nod and hand June the knife I pulled off the other zombie and holster the gun. I still have the tire iron.

"We've got five Zs," I call to Dallas as we get in sight of her. "Can you help us out?"

She nods and runs up to us, the stick I gave her in one hand and a big rock in the other. She doesn't look scared, not really, more tense. She looks like June does. Me, my stomach is doing backflips, but it does this every time I have to face a Z. Every time.

One bite and it's a guaranteed awful ending. A broken leg and you're done. Sprain your ankle, and that's probably going to be the end too.

I'm not really a warrior. I mean, I fight, like hell, when I have to, but I would just as soon not have to. The look on the two women's faces make me think they are both warriors. I'm not saying they're not scared, that they don't worry about the same things that I do. I just feel like they have that warrior spirit that I lack.

And gender norms be damned, I'm glad to have them. The zombie apocalypse did away with all that crap. When zombies are bearing down on you, you want warriors, man or woman doesn't matter a bit.

Well, that's true with us and with Talia's group, but probably not with the psychotic, petty, wannabe warlord in Flagstaff. Those dudes seemed to be going in the opposite direction.

"You two," June says to us, "stay behind me a bit."

The Zs snarl and snap and lurch towards us, the dank rotting smell of them filling my nose. We lead them out onto the wider main road, their attention focused on June who is the closest one to them.

This causes them to not be five Zs shoulder to shoulder, but a loose line of them. I see what she's doing, thinning them out a bit; they don't all move at the same pace.

We make our way down the road in the direction of the visitor's center and lodge, staying about five yards away from them. In a few minutes, they are a single-file line with a big burly male zombie in the lead, and a flannel-shirted female right behind him. The other three have fallen a few seconds behind. Both of the lead zombies have backpacks on and show minimal damage. They're recent zombies and a bit slow for it, the fungus not having as good control over them as it soon will.

I come up even with June and see that Dallas does the same. "Now?"

June sheaths her knife and pulls her gun. "Now."

I rush the big guy and swing the tire iron hard, connecting the thicker, bent end with his head.

I am dimly aware of Dallas taking on the female Z, but don't have any attention to spare.

My blow is glancing and he stumbles, but no real damage done. I am so missing my baseball bat, I would have taken him out with one swing.

I dance back, my foot catching on a crack in the pavement and I almost go down, my attention away from the zombie and on staying upright.

When I look back up, the snapping jaw of the Z is too damn close, but suddenly he is pulled back. It's Dallas, who grabs him by his backpack and yanks him, giving me the moment I need. I rush in and shove the pointed end of the tire iron through his eye socket and he goes down.

The female Z is down and then June is there with her knife and it's three living versus three dead.

These are good odds. My butterflies are gone, my breath coming fast, my heart beating hard. The butterflies have been replaced with the adrenaline of survival. I don't think of Talia or that impending threat, I don't worry about how little we know about Dallas, I don't even think of the future I so want to have with June. It's just the fight now, just survival.

We spread out a bit, a Z heading towards each of us, mine a young man with a scruffy brown beard and a beanie askew on his head, greasy black hair sticking out.

I go in with the tire iron ready. I let him grab me and pull me towards him. I use that momentum and shove the sharp end in his eye as hard as I can... and he goes down.

I look up and June has a middle-aged female zombie she is working with. She rushes in, aims a kick at the Z's knee and then rushes out. Smart.

I look for Dallas and she's in trouble. A big male Z is on her and she seems to have lost both her weapons, which were just a rock and a hastily sharpened stick, for which I feel bad.

I rush over and grab him by the backpack and yank him off her. The Z goes down and I stomp on his chest and swing hard with the tire iron. It makes a mess, unleashing a fungal funk as his head splits open, but it does the job.

I look up and June is on top of her Z, her knife flashing down to its head.

And then Dallas is on me. Hugging me hard, pressing her not insubstantial curves against me.

"Thank you, thank you," she whispers breathlessly. "I... It..." She's shaking, and even though she has that warrior vibe, I can't say I blame her. She was under equipped and was in a bad spot.

"Yeah... Sure... Thanks for your help." I pat her on the back.

I can smell her sweat and the funk of the zombie, but I have to say it feels nice to have her pressed against me. And I feel bad that it feels nice. But I was alone for many months, and she is attractive, and it is only natural.

I had one post-apocalyptic relationship, and let's just say that it ended rather badly.

Dallas is sniffing and I can see June staring at us. The look on her face is hard to read, one eyebrow raised a bit, her lips pursed, her brow furrowed, but not in that decidedly cute way.

I try to give June a "what can I do?" look and open my arms so it's clear who is hugging who.

"I owe you my life, Woody," Dallas says. "Seriously. I'm... I'm forever in your debt."

I slowly push her away and connect with her brown eyes. She seems sincere.

"Any time, Dallas," I say. "You helped me, I helped you." I shrug and walk over towards June, making my eyes wide, to kind of say "what the hell," but she's not looking at me. She's examining the Z she took down and suddenly I'm worried. Does June think I like Dallas? And with another woman around will I ever have the conversation with June that we need to have?

But I shake all that romantic crap off. It's still survival time and we need to figure out what's going on with these new Zs and find a way out of here.

CHAPTER EIGHT

WE'VE ENCOUNTERED six zombies since we got here. Four of them have backpacks, all of them seem to be new Zs. This is a stroke of good fortune—for us, not for this poor recently alive group. It's lucky because backpacks mean supplies when we had little chance of finding any up here.

It's also a mystery. How did they get here? How did they die? Six equipped humans can handle quite a few Zs in an isolated environment like this, especially this late in the zombie game.

We're all standing there breathing deeply of the cool air, staring at the bodies, the silence again feeling sudden and somehow ominous. A place like this, there should be noise.

Both June and Dallas are looking at me. Somehow, I am the leader, because I have the most knowledge of the area, although I suspect both of them are better trained for it than I am.

June was in the Army. Dallas was... well, she was part of Talia's Phantom Company, but I wouldn't be surprised to learn that she has some military training too.

"Okay," I say, trying to get my brain moving. "Let's get anything usable off them and let's find out how they turned. These Zs are new and that is bothering me."

I can't say that I trust Dallas at this point, but it seems like it's time to give her some more autonomy and get her better equipped. June is keeping her distance from Dallas and that's just fine.

There's no more talking and we all get to work on these five Zs and I go back and drag over the one that I took care of on the way in, shooing the ravens away that were having a meal.

We pull backpacks, jackets, shirts, knives, belts, guns, canteens, and search pockets. We even find a couple of life-straw portable water filters, a bigger hand-pump water filter, and a hunting rifle that June claims. I get a pair of boots my size, and we get their socks—they'll need to be washed, but hey, socks can make all the difference when you are on the move all the time.

A group of ravens have taken up residence in the pine trees around us and are cawing up a storm. They're hungry, they want us to leave the Zs to them. In some ways this is comforting, the circle of life continues. In other ways it's just creepy, all these big birds with shiny black feathers and big beaks staring at the proceedings.

We've got a pile of the usable gear off to the side and the Zs are down to their skivvies—no one seems interested in inheriting zombie underwear (except for the socks). We all have our limits.

"How did they die?" I ask.

We stand there gazing at the pale but nearly normal-looking bodies. The heads are a mess from our fight, but the rest of them look... normal. Entirely normal. The normal scrapes and cuts and bruises you'd see on anyone living out of doors. No bites, beyond bug bites. No gunshot wounds. Nothing out of the ordinary.

"Shit," June says.

"What the..." Dallas adds in.

"This is not good," I say.

Suddenly we have a problem bigger than if we can trust Dallas or if Talia is coming after June or even if June likes me.

We have new zombies that don't have any bite marks or other obvious causes of death.

We might just have a new way that humans turn.

Shit.

CHAPTER NINE

"ZOMBIE 101," I begin, pacing on the paved road to the North Rim lodge in front of the stripped-down zombie bodies, scraping my foot on the debris time has deposited. "We all know this, but maybe saying it will jar something loose."

June and Dallas nod.

"First, zombies are driven by a parasitic, fungal infection, source unknown." I throw June a smile, but she's not having any of it.

"Fungal?" Dallas asks.

I nod and detour, explaining how old zombies have a white mass in their skulls that looks like a big head of cauliflower and white threads of fungal fiber running throughout their bodies. I tell Dallas about the dissection June and I did on the South Rim.

"Okay," I continue, "fungus-head zombies driven by a parasitic infection that we all have. We die, we turn into a zombie. We get bit and zombie spit in the blood stream supercharges the infection and we die and then turn into a zombie. I also think that if we ingest too much zombie goo... you know, blood, splattered brains, etcetera... well, you get the picture." I stop and point at the arrayed corpses. "No bite marks, they're not covered in recent zombie splatter, something else killed them, but what?"

"Virus?" Dallas offers.

"Infection?" June says.

"Right. Something all six of them were exposed to. Either they all ingested it or it was communicable. And that means..."

"We better hope for ingestion," June says.

"Because if it was a contagion," Dallas says, biting her thumbnail, "we are all so very screwed."

I nod. "So next step, see if they have a camp around here, see if we can find something they might all have ingested. And that means, we can't eat their food or drink their water."

We had found some canned goods, dried fruit, and even a couple power bars in their packs. We are all hungry, so not eating is a big sacrifice. Not drinking, an even bigger deal.

"And we need to find water," June says. Her lips are chapped as are all of ours. It is, fortunately, not hot, but we are getting more and more dehydrated, and how these people died won't matter if we don't get water pretty soon.

I look up at the sky through the pine trees. We have about two hours before the sun goes down and it gets cold. "And we need shelter," I add.

I don't say that we need to get out of here and get away from Talia and Phantom Company. That doesn't need saying.

Without further discussion, the three of us head back past the physical plant and to the water tanks where June and I had encountered the Zs. We all have knives on our belts, but June snagged the two guns the Zs had on them, so Dallas doesn't have a firearm. Not trust yet, but more of a "bigger fish to fry right now" kind of a thing.

The camp doesn't take long to find, it is in the woods just behind the water tanks. Three tents outfitted with propane lanterns, air mattresses, and sleeping bags.

My first thought is, wow, luxury. My next thought is, that is way too much crap to be hauling around when zombies are chasing you.

June is close, her elbow brushing mine as we approach through the fir trees. She's got her gun out and I've got the tire iron in hand. Dallas is a few yards to our left with a knife in hand as if she understands the temporary truce we have here with trust.

"A van!" Dallas says, and runs right through the camp before we've had a chance to check it for the living and the dead.

It's an old white cargo van that was driven around the water tanks and hidden behind some trees. She opens the door; the light comes on and it dings a warning that the keys are in the ignition.

"It's got half a tank of gas," she calls back excitedly.

My brain freezes. This is what we need. Gear and escape from Talia. But, what happened here? I don't want to fall into the same trap these folks did—provided that it's even avoidable.

"Should we..." I begin nodding towards Dallas and the van.

June shakes her head. "Let her leave if that's what she wants, but I don't think it is." She ends up looking at me pointedly.

I hold my hands up. "Hey, that hug thing was all her."

A brief smile plays on her lips. "Don't pretend you didn't enjoy it."

I feel my cheeks flush. "I won't. But she's not who I want to be with."

And here it is. Another potential moment. June's deep blue eyes lock with mine, no danger falling on us this very moment, the sweet smell of pine and fir trees in the air, the cool breeze playing with her short black hair, and then...

Hooooonk. "Come on, guys!" Dallas yells. "Let's get the hell out of here before Phantom Company gets here."

I sigh and June chuckles.

"Hold on," I yell. "We need to figure out what happened."

Now that I'm not lost in the deep blue ocean of June's eyes, I can smell something dank just underneath the sweet vanillay pine trees and the sharper scent of the firs.

"What? Are you kidding me!?" Dallas yells.

"Better go explain it to your girlfriend," June says, but I can see the smile on her face. "And get her to stop making so much noise."

Shaking my head, I walk over to give Dallas the news.

CHAPTER TEN

"SO... why didn't you just kiss her," Dallas asks, her voice low and conspiratorial when I get over to the van. The window is rolled down and she's in the driver's seat leaning towards me, a smile playing on her full lips.

"It's complicated," I say.

"It wouldn't be for me," she says, her eyes looking me up and down and my heart pounding hard. "Seriously, it wouldn't be complicated, Woody."

I sigh.

"Things are so uncertain, I'd have fun whenever I could if I could land a good guy like you."

"Dallas..."

"Come on, I'm not repulsive, although I haven't had a bath in a while." She takes a sniff at one of her armpits and wrinkles her nose rather comically.

"Look, we are going to try to figure out what happened to these six. Can you—"

"If we were a thing," she says, cutting me off, "we'd be in this van celebrating being alive right now."

My jaw is agape and I am sure I look like a fool, my heart now pounding in my ears.

"Right now," she whispers, leaning even closer, and I can smell her sweaty scent. It's not altogether bad and she's not altogether unattractive and I am healthy enough to be feeling exactly what she wants me to be feeling.

Seconds tick by in slow motion and we're just there, our faces close, her brown eyes wide, her face dead serious. My body at war with my mind.

My meeting with June was wary and comical, this Dallas is aggressive and... Well, I'm not sure exactly what she is, and part of my logical brain—the part that is barely functioning—knows this may all be part of Talia's plan to get me away from June.

"We... I..." I stammer.

Dallas laughs and shakes her head and then louder says, "Sure, Woody, I'll help search the camp." And then quieter she adds, "The offer stands, Mr. Beckman, any time you want to take me up on it... anytime, anywhere."

CHAPTER ELEVEN

IT'S like the world has changed or something as we all search the camp. I notice how tight Dallas's tank-top is and how generously endowed she is, how strong her long legs are. I mean, I noticed all that before, but now I really *notice*. I see her smile lines as cute and her brown eyes as soulful.

Stupid, I know. Biology in action, nothing more, but that doesn't negate the powerful hormones in biology's arsenal, and Dallas sure knew how to use those weapons.

I find myself isolating from the two women, facing away so I can't see either of them while I search. Seeing June makes me feel guilty and seeing Dallas makes me feel... well, I think you get the picture.

The camp has the three tents, a fire ring, some pots and pans for cooking, and a hatchet. It's perched just beyond the water tank before the hill drops steeply off, the tents situated where the trees allow but in sight of each other. I grab the hatchet and shove the handle into my belt. If I can't have a bat, a hatchet is much more appealing than a tire iron.

"Over here," June calls.

She's at the back of the water tank closest to camp where there are some large pipes and valves.

"They were collecting water here," June says when I get close, pointing to a large pipe jutting out of the bottom of the dull-green tank, with a big valve, a 90-degree turn pointing the open end down. It is slowly dripping water into a metal pot that's overflowing.

"Smart," I say.

June looks up, her eyes serious and she shakes her head, pointing to the pipe which has long bone-white tendrils of something coming out. Each drip of water slides down a tendril into the bucket. Drip. Drip. Drip.

The tendrils are maybe an inch long and look remarkably like the fungus we found running through the arm of the zombie we dissected. I squat down by June and look in the pipe—it's full of the white stuff and my nose fills with the heavy fungal funk of it, the source of the dank scent I smelled earlier.

I stand up and step back, suddenly hot, and look up at the water tanks. The fungus spores must have gotten in there and thrived in the moist, closed atmosphere.

"Shit!" I say. Not eloquent, I know, but I have no other words.

"So what's the deal over here?" Dallas asks, sauntering up, and I am thankful that the fear of fungal parasite hormones has totally swamped the horny young man hormones.

"Fungus water," I say, pointing at the large pipe, which must be some sort of emergency drain. I rub at my nose which is still full of the stench I sucked in while up close. "They drank fungus water. I guess it killed them."

Dallas is staring at the white strands, blinking. "Before... before you told me about the fungus-heads, I would have... I would have drunk that water."

June nods solemnly and gets up, looking at me.

"Okay," I say with a sigh, trying to get my head back in the game. "Grab the sleeping bags and lanterns, let's load up the van and get the hell out of here."

"No tents?" Dallas asks, giving me a look that I am sure is meant to be sultry, but the fungus-creeps are still with me.

"In a zombie apocalypse, tents are dumb. We need to see the Zs coming."

"Right," Dallas says with a nod and then raises her middle finger and points it to the south. "We are out of here, Phantom Company and crazy Talia. Eat me!" She whoops and runs to a tent and starts pulling gear out.

I'm staring at Dallas, and beside me June sighs.

"What were you and your girlfriend talking about for so long?" June asks.

I look at her and there is no smile there this time.

"She... I..." My face is red and my blood pressure is going up, yet again.

"I need to know, Woody. Seriously."

Dallas has her arms loaded with sleeping bags and is running towards the van, chanting obscenities at Talia.

"She offered me... umm... herself," I say. I don't know how else to put it. I don't know if it was a relationship she was offering, or even what a relationship would be like with Dallas.

June's eyes look sad and she smiles weakly. "Ahh... I thought so."

"What?" I began. "How could you—"

"Oh, please, Woody. She couldn't have been telegraphing it more obviously if she had been wearing a T-shirt that said, 'Take me, Woody.'"

I shake my head, dumbfounded. I didn't really see it. And that makes me wonder what I'm missing with June.

"Everything I said to you stands," I say to June.

She smiles, her blue eyes brighter. "And that makes you a smart man."

My mouth is moving, but I don't know what to say.

"Talia," she whispers, taking my hand and squeezing it. "I don't know if this is all Dallas, all Talia, or something in between."

She lets go of my hand, walks to the nearest tent, and starts pulling gear out.

I take a stone and scratch the word "TOXIC" on the pipe to hopefully keep more people from dying. Phantom Company may still be using it and as much as I hate Talia, there are some good people down there. As I squat there, my nose stinging from the strength of the moldy-fungus smell, I realize that closed water stores like this, all over the country, probably have the same thing happening. A new wave of zombies is rising up right now.

I then write "TOXIC" in large letters on the back of both water tanks. It's not much, but it's something, at least.

After I'm done, I watch the two of them for just a few seconds, before shaking my head and joining them.

CHAPTER TWELVE

THERE IS ONLY one paved road out of the North Rim of the Grand Canyon, Route 67. It runs about forty-five miles from the Canyon north to Jacob Lake across the Kaibab Plateau.

The land is gorgeous, rolling grass meadows flanked with fir/spruce forests with a sprinkling of aspen and pine trees. As dusk settles in, we drive through a burned-out section of the forest, the opportunistic aspens first up after the fire, short and thick, the scared trunks of the taller trees ghostly among them. It looks and feels post-apocalyptic, and I guess it really is. The fire was the apocalypse, the new aspen forest, although far too dense, is the beginning for the "post" apocalypse. The forest will be different, but it's returning. It's grim, but it somehow gives me hope.

By the time we get to Jacob Lake, it's dark. Our journey was slowed by several wrecks in the road we had to scout and slowly get around.

On the way, June peppered Dallas with questions such as: Does Phantom Company have vehicles and gas stores at the ready on the North Rim?—yes, but she had no idea where. How far do they range to the north?—they have been to Fredonia, but met another group in

Kanab and one in Colorado City and haven't been farther. What kind of force would likely come after them?—enough to get the job done.

All of this made Jacob Lake not a great place to stop, but we needed to stop. We had eaten the power bars now that we were pretty sure the fungus water had killed them, but we had left all their water, fearing that it was contaminated.

Jacob Lake is at eight thousand feet in the middle of a ponderosa pine forest. The stop isn't much more than a gas station—and we need gas—a gift shop, restaurant, and inn, a visitor's center, and a campground.

There are enough cars here so that I'm not worried about a random van being spotted. Going down a forest service road would be more discrete, but then we would be easily trapped. Here there are multiple escape routes.

The gas station is old-fashioned with a flat-roof covering the pumps and a single-vehicle garage, the only one around for many miles.

I pull up to the edge of the roof and say, "Let's figure out how to get up there for the night. Even if they come, they won't be able to see us."

June smiles and eyes the height. We found some rope in the van so if we can get someone up there, we can all get up there. It won't make for a fast getaway, but it has been a couple of days since June and I have slept, and we need rest.

"What?" Dallas says. "That's just..." She trails off when she sees our faces.

"We like roofs," I say, smiling at June.

"Oh, get a room, you two... please!"

CHAPTER THIRTEEN

EVEN STANDING on top of the van, the roof is too high, but the rope is long enough to lob over the short side, get it tied to one of the poles, and from the roof of the van, June scrambles up.

"Well?" I yell up.

June appears on the edge, her hands on her hips, illuminated by the lanterns we've got going. "It'll work. We can get the rope anchored up here and then pull it up after everyone and everything is up."

It takes about an hour to haul all the gear up and stash the van in front of the inn, where it hopefully won't be noticed. I even unhook the battery, open the van door, and toss a bunch of pine needles in and dirty up the windshield so it looks like all the other vehicles. I kick around the debris in the parking lot so it's not obvious I just drove it there. I'm last to climb up, and with the van gone, I have to climb all the way up the rope. It's not as high as the dog food plant in Flagstaff, but in my diminished state, it's a challenge despite the knots we put in the rope.

After I'm up, we pull up the rope and gather around a single lantern right in the middle of the metal roof. Comfortable, it's not, but it's safe from Zs and hidden from the living.

The night is cold and the sleeping bags are welcome as we sit there. Dallas hands me an open can of green beans with a fork in it, and I gratefully get all the moisture out of it I can.

It helps, but it's not enough. I've got that spiking pain in my head that is a warning that dehydration is going to get serious soon.

June pulls her gun out and points it at Dallas. "Time to tell us everything."

I didn't know she was going to do this and my tired body dumps more adrenaline in my bloodstream. Not much, but some. Enough to, weirdly, make me feel even more tired as my heart beats hard.

Above, the Milky Way is strewn over us and I wish I could just lie down, hold June's hand, and stare at the stars for the ten seconds it would take me to fall asleep.

"I have told you the truth," Dallas says dryly, as if she doesn't believe she's in real danger. I know June a little better than she does and am quite sure she *is* in real danger.

"Not all of it," June says calmly as if she's commenting on the weather in San Diego—yes, it's going to be yet another beautiful, sunny day.

"All of it," Dallas says.

"Bullshit." June cocks the gun.

"Is this about me taking a shot with your boy toy?"

My adrenalized mind is spinning, this is not the kind of thing you want to get into the middle of, but I don't want any lives to end here tonight.

Even if Dallas is here to split June and me up, not that I can say we are truly "together"... Okay, that's not fair. We are partners, we have been working as a team. We are "together," just not in the sense of being a couple.

"Why don't you just tell us what happened last night," I offer. "Go slow. Give us all the details."

I try to catch June's eye, but she is focused on Dallas.

Dallas takes a deep breath and sighs. "I was on sentry duty at the Kaibab Bridge, there are two sentries on each of those at all times. I was with Trent, who has the annoying habit of watching me more than the bridge, even in the dark. He's way too old for me and just stinks of desperation. Anyway, we both see the unusual flicker of light from The Ranch a little after 2:00 a.m. and I knew it was you guys and I knew it meant you were trying to escape.

"Talia talked about you," Dallas nods towards June and in fact her gaze has been fixed on June the whole time. It doesn't seem to matter at all that I'm here. "I knew that you were smart and tough and I knew that this was my chance. So, I left Trent, telling him it was a fire and he'd have to watch all on his own."

"Don't you have walkie talkies?" June asks. "Didn't you check in first before leaving? Didn't Trent?"

She smiles and shakes her head. "No, and I took the walkie with me and ditched it later. Trent isn't the brightest bulb."

June nods for her to continue.

Dallas shrugs and glances at me briefly. "I liked the look of you too, so I took a chance and followed. I saw your standoff, freezing my ass off in the creek. After Talia, Sal, and Harris left, I waited a while and followed."

She shrugs as if that explains everything, but it really doesn't. This could be the truth, this could be a lie. Maybe that's what the shrug is about—take it or leave it, I can't prove it anyway.

June sighs and shakes her head. My eyes burn I'm so tired and my headache is even worse. It has been less than twenty-four hours since we set that fire at Phantom Ranch and a lot has happened. We are all exhausted.

The silence just hangs there, thick and nearly tangible. June and Dallas staring at each other as if it's some kind of contest.

"I wish we could believe you," I finally say, because I can't stand the tension. "But Talia could have told you all that and sent you on after us."

Dallas meets my eyes, the lantern putting her look of distaste in rough relief. "I hate that bitch," Dallas spits out. "Risking my life like this, chasing you with no weapon, no water..." She shakes her head and holds up her scraped hand. "No. I wouldn't do that for Talia." She sighs, her shoulders falling, and suddenly she looks as tired as I feel. "I left food, shelter, and security to take a chance with you two. I'm sorry you can't see it."

And then she's crying. Not like at the Supai Tunnel, this time it's a quieter, more controlled weeping, her eyes flicking between me and June. I feel that weird knee-jerk need to do something to make it stop, but I shove it down and just sit there, my mouth dry, my head hurting, and my eyes heavy.

It doesn't go on, she soon wraps her sleeping bag tight around her and lies down.

I look at June, wondering what the hell we do now. We can't let her go, even if she isn't working for Talia; she might run right back to her.

"I'll take first watch and wake you in a few hours," June says. I open my mouth to object and she cuts me off. "Just get some sleep, Woody. We're all too tired to think."

I nod and lie down on the hard roof and stare up at the Milky Way, bright and sparkling above us. It takes me far less than ten seconds to fall asleep.

CHAPTER FOURTEEN

MY MOUTH IS dry and my eyes thick with sleep as consciousness slowly returns. At first it feels like a dream, just a brief bit of pre-apocalypse paranoia. I can hear people talking about me, the noise of it like buzzing flies I just want to shoo away.

I'm back in my bed in Phoenix in a two-bedroom apartment I share with two other guys. I'm enrolled in community college taking business and accounting courses, waiting tables to pay the bills, trying to claw my way out of minimum wage work.

We all had different hours in that cramped, thin-walled apartment, and I often heard people talking about me while I was sleeping. My half-asleep brain would hear my name and imagine that they were saying bad things about me, that each laugh was at my expense. I hated it, but I wasn't about to go crawling back to Mom and Dad and sleep in my old room, which had been converted into a workout room with a treadmill that no one used.

My hip and shoulder hurt and the air has a cold bite to it and I realize that I'm not stuck in the mundane treadmill of making money, paying bills, and trying to sneak in some fun. I'm a survivor in a post-apocalypse America on a different kind of treadmill. Fight zombies, avoid the living, survive, laugh a little to make life worth living.

My eyes flutter open and I see the tops of pine trees and a grey clouded sky behind them, illuminated by the pre-dawn light. My breath puffs out in condensate in front of me.

"Put that damn gun down," I hear a female voice say. It's a bit deep and speaks the order as if it's used to being obeyed. "We don't want to alert them to our presence if they're still here."

"But, sir," a gruff male voice says, "the deer. We could use the meat."

My brain begins to engage as I slowly, regretfully, wake all the way up. Both voices are familiar.

"I swear to God, Sal, with Jesus as my witness above and Gaia below, I will beat you senseless where you stand if you keep questioning my orders."

Talia!

I sit up and suck in a breath, my not-quite-awake brain getting ready to sound the alarm when a cold hand is clamped over my mouth.

"Don't. Say. A word," June hisses in my ear.

Fully awake, I nod and she takes her hand off my mouth and I look around. Dallas is sitting there, her brown hair disheveled, her eyes wide, a sleeping bag still around her body.

June's blue eyes look filled with sleep too, and she's sitting up in a sleeping bag, the fatigue must have gotten her while she watched and she fell asleep too.

"Goddamn Dallas," Talia says from below us, the sound of her combat boots smacking on the pavement a steady rhythm. "I gave that girl one thing to do. Distract a horny boy. How hard is that?" There's a pause, and the tapping of boots stop. "Well, Sal, how goddamn hard is that?"

June's nostrils flare and she slowly pulls the gun out of her sleeping bag and points it at Dallas in a "we might all be screwed, but you'll be first" kind of gesture.

There is a sloshing sound and the distinct scent of gas fumes.

"Wouldn't think it be hard," Sal said, "seeing how he was still in his twenties and... Shit!"

"What!?" Talia asks.

"Oh. False alarm," Sal says. "All good. Plenty of gas left and no sign of the lock being tampered with. Just some air in the line."

"Well, where the hell are they?" Talia says. "Dallas was under strict orders to not let them get any farther than Jacob Lake."

Dallas is hugging her chest with her arms, her head down, her eyes not meeting either of ours.

We don't move. We hardly breathe, until we hear Talia and Sal get in a pickup truck and drive away.

Then June cocks the gun and points it at Dallas's head.

CHAPTER FIFTEEN

WHAT OFFENSE CAN one human do to another that justifies murder in cold blood? Justifies as in "just," as in right, as in something you can live with. And by "live with" I mean be able to sleep at night.

Hell if I know.

Dallas has certainly danced near that line with us, but has she crossed it?

"I told you the truth," Dallas says after the truck is out of the area. "I did try to escape. I did witness your little showdown where Talia threatened to blow your boyfriend's brains out." The girls are once again having a conversation between them, and while I am the object of much of it, it doesn't really matter that I am here.

I can't say that I like the feeling all that much.

"But Talia caught me after you two left," Dallas continues. "She was so mad, but she's smart. She heard about me noticing Woody in the mess hall—everyone's a gossip down there—so she told me that if I took care of Woody then I could have my freedom."

"Took care of me?" I ask.

Dallas looks at me, but only briefly as if I am some kind of annoyance in all of this. "She was very specific that I should not kill you unless I had to, that would leave you martyred to June and she would forever wonder what might have been."

"And we can't have that, can we," I say, injecting as much sarcasm as I can into the phrase. And given the headache and dehydration and hunger, it isn't all that much. But she's not paying attention to me anyway.

"And what of the leverage we established against Talia in what you call our 'stand off'?" June asks.

The leverage was that June knew of Talia's messy past in Afghanistan and what had happened in Albuquerque with her jealousy and the band she led there post-apocalypse. (Maybe I should just start abbreviating that as post-A, it's a little long and I'm tired of writing it.) The leverage is how we got Talia to let us leave.

"Yeah. That," Dallas says with a smirk. "I asked Talia and she told me she was going to 'confess' to the entire Company as soon she got back."

I'm staring, a question on my face. I have clearly missed something.

June throws me a wry smile. "Talia was going to get ahead of it and tell her side of the story, which will be incomplete, at the least, and make her come out looking very good."

I shake my head, those psychotic, petty, wannabe warlords have a lot of tricks up their sleeves. This time, the "psychotic" part of it being at the forefront. They are definitely part of the "ends justifies the means" crowd.

"And what means will she use to find us?" June asks.

Dallas shrugs. "It would be a guess."

June gestures casually with her gun. "So, guess."

"Talia will go back before the end of today. Phantom Company means more to her than you do, and she never leaves for too long. After that, she'll send a small team after you, probably led by Harris. He's..." Her face gets this faraway look and then her lips purse in a sour expression. "He's good. He'll find you."

June nods, her face hard, not betraying any emotions. Me? I'd just as soon pee my pants, but I'm too damn dehydrated.

"And what should I do with you?" June asks.

The question surprises me, and judging by Dallas's expression, it surprises her too.

She's silent for a long time before she says, "No matter what I say, you can't trust my motives. If the situation was reversed, I'd kill you, but I wouldn't use that gun with them in the area."

June nods slowly. "Stand up. Hold your hands high. Turn your back to me."

I want to say something, but my mouth is so dry and I just can't think.

Dallas does as she is told.

June slowly walks up to her and says quietly, "You know, I like you. I wish this could be different."

"Likewise," Dallas says.

With that, June slowly releases the hammer on the gun, grabs the gun by the barrel, and hits Dallas hard on the head with the butt.

Dallas goes down in a heap.

My mouth is open, I am trying to speak, when June's blue eyes meet mine.

"Don't worry," she says. "We're not like them."

CHAPTER SIXTEEN

AS THE SUN crests the horizon, the thin orange glow is harsh on my tired eyes, we move quickly. I make sure Dallas is still breathing and tie her up. We leave her a can of food, her backpack, and sleeping bag.

We're not like them.

This is the thought that keeps bouncing around my head, keeps me fighting through the dehydration. The air is cool and my limbs don't quite obey me at first, but it gets better as I warm up.

We're not like them.

I sneak a few looks at June, and if I was taken with her before, well, it's an entirely different thing now. She has retained her humanity which, right at that moment, seems more important than survival, and sexier too.

On top of the can of peas, I put the sharp metal lid to the can we had last night. She can use it to cut through her rope, albeit a little slowly.

We are giving her a chance.

I slide down the rope and pull the van around. I use the tire iron and break through the lock to the gas tanks, use the ball pump and tubing that was in the van to pump the tank full and three plastic gas cans that were in there.

June slides down the rope and lands on top of the van, cuts the rope and throws it back up top.

Dallas will have a six-foot drop getting down. Her feet will sting like hell, but it will be doable. I put her knife on top of one of the gas pumps; she'll need it if she's to survive.

June and I do all this with very little conversation. Talia is out here. We have to find another place to hide before Dallas wakes up or anyone from Phantom Company comes back around.

For the moment, our plan is simple. Head out into the forest service roads, find a cow tank, I know they are out here, and get some water. Stay ahead of Phantom Company.

We're not like them.

Suddenly I am no longer wondering whether June likes me or anything like that. It just doesn't matter. June and I are a "we." I'll happily take whatever that means.

In the van, June cracks open a can of black beans and we slowly eat it, careful to get every bit of moisture. Even that little bit of water clears my head some and I suddenly feel optimistic, like there is actually a chance for June and me.

I grin at her as I start the van up. "How many zombies does it take to woo the girl?" I ask.

She opens her mouth as if to speak and then her brow furrows, her beautiful eyes meeting mine and her face softening. "Not gonna happen, they lack the *braainnnss*," she offers, punctuating it with a little giggle.

"Well, yeah, but that's not it," I say.

She shrugs. "Well, I don't know then. How many zombies *does* it take to woo the girl?"

"They can't do it," I say with a smile. "She's got her heart set on a baseball-obsessed guy named Woody from Phoenix, Arizona."

She's quiet for a moment and my heart leaps thinking I've misjudged the situation. She's just not into me. She's only staying because she needs me to survive—ha, as if! And then she slowly nods, her eyes connecting with mine again. "Yup, that's about the size of it."

I pull us out of Jacob Lake and head onto 89A to the east with the biggest smile in the post-apocalyptic world on my face.

Sure, we've got June's obsessed ex on our trail, God knows what Dallas will be like when she wakes up, and the entire undead population of the Desert Southwest would love to snack on us, but June and I are a "we."

And that is a lot pre- or post-apocalypse.

EPISODE 6

WOODY AND JUNE VERSUS PHANTOM COMPANY

More adventure, so much more danger, and a lot more Woody and June awaits you in.... *Woody and June versus the June versus the Phantom Company*.

Coming soon on August 14, 2019

Join the Woody and June Fan Club at WoodyAndJune.com so you don't miss a thing (plus fun behind-the-scenes features and free stuff!).

WOODY AND JUNE VERSUS PHANTOM COMPANY

Desperate Times Call for Foolish Measures

When Woody Beckman meets June Medina, neither expects the adventures that will follow. Dedicated go-it-alone survivors, they've learned not to trust anyone in post-zombie-apocalypse Arizona, except each other.

When outmanned and overpowered by a trained paramilitary

group, can Woody and June find a way to survive, much less stay together? Can the mercurial Dallas be trusted?

Can Woody and June survive the humans, escape the unforgiving desert, and find out if there is really anything between them?

A story of adventure and love and taking things (even the apocalypse) in stride.

ABOUT THE AUTHOR

Robert J. McCarter is the author of six novels, three novellas, and dozens of short stories. He is a finalist for the *Writers of the Future* contest and his stories have appeared in *The Saturday Evening Post, Adomeda Spaceways Inflight Magazine, Everyday Fiction,* and numerous anthologies.

He has written a series of first person ghost novels (starting with Shuffled Off: A Ghost's Memoir) and a superhero / love story series (Neutrinoman and Lightningirl, A Love Story), as well as two short story collections.

Of his latest novel, *Seeing Forever,* Kirkus Reviews says, "Sci-fi as it should be: engaging, moving, and grand in scope."

Find out more at:
robertjmccarter.com

BOOKS BY ROBERT J. MCCARTER

WOODY AND JUNE VERSUS THE APOCALYPSE

1. Woody and June versus the Wannabe Warlord
2. Woody and June versus the Fungus-Head Zombies
3. Woody and June versus the Grand Canyon
4. Woody and June versus the Ex
5. Woody and June versus the Third Wheel
6. Woody and June versus Phantom Company (*coming August, 2019*)
7. Woody and June versus the Daring Rescue (*coming September, 2019*)

Join the Woody and June Fan Club at WoodyAndJune.com

NOVELS IN THE "GHOST'S MEMOIR" WORLD:

- Shuffled Off: A Ghost's Memoir, Book 1
- Drawing the Dead
- To Be a Fool: A Ghost's Memoir, Book 2
- Of Things Not Seen: A Ghost's Memoir, Book 3

OTHER NOVELS:

- Seeing Forever

BOOKS IN THE NEUTRINOMAN AND LIGHTNINGIRL SERIES:

- Meteor Attack! Neutrinoman and Lightningirl, A Love Story. Episode 1
- Toxic Asset: Neutrinoman and Lightningirl, A Love Story. Episode 2
- Protocol X: Neutrinoman and Lightningirl, A Love Story. Episode 3
- Season 1 (Omnibus edition of Episodes 1 - 3)
- Off Book: Neutrinoman and Lightningirl, A Love Story. Episode 4 (*Coming soon*)

WALTER ANCHOR, GHOST DETECTIVE STORIES

- **Case 1: "Detecting Haley"** (part of *Life After: Stories of Life, Death, and the Places in Between*)
- **Case 2: "The Ghost Brides Gift"** (exclusive to newsletter subscribers)
- **Case 3: "A Long Hard Fall"** (coming in 2019)

For a complete list of Walter Anchor stories, go to RobertJMcCarter.com/WalterAnchor

SHORT STORES AND COLLECTIONS

- Life After: Stories of Life, Death, and the Places in Between
- Anomalous Readings: Thirteen Curious and Confounding Tales
- Probability: Resolve
- The Turing Test Will Be Televised

- Ghost Hacker, Zombie Maker

  For a complete list, go to RobertJMcCarter.com

www.ingramcontent.com/pod-product-compliance
Lightning Source LLC
Chambersburg PA
CBHW020317150626
46552CB00022B/2918